**To Douglas**, for all the gentle nudges to finish this book and for believing in me and what I am trying to do. You are my biggest fan and I couldn't (and wouldn't) be doing this without you.

**To Lou, the best big brother ever**. Thanks for being under the big mimosa tree when I jumped, on the other side of the creek when I was swinging across, and flying up to DC on "business" when I got into my own "jams." I was so fortunate to have you for my Big Brother while I was growing up…and still am.

**To Jared and Cameron**, the two most special little boys ever…may you be as close growing up as me and your Uncle Lou, and may you figure out how to get out of all of your own jams. You are both so precious to me. YOU are my MAGIC!

*I Love You, Rainey*

Published by:
**DreamDog Press**
3686 King Street, Suite 160
Alexandria, VA  22302

Order DreamDog Adventure Products:
1-877-2-RAINEY
1-877-272-4639
or online at:
**www.dreamdog.com**

Copyright © 2002 by Lorraine Friedman
Illustrated by Betsy Dill
Art Direction and Cover Layout by Doug Hamann

Publisher's Cataloging-in-Publication
(Provided by Quality Books, Inc.)

Friedman, Lorraine
    Jerome's jam/ by Rainey ; illustrated by Betsy Dill.
    --1st ed.
    p. cm.
    SUMMARY: Rhyming story about a new baby coming to Jerome's family and how jealousy turns into the wonderful fun of being a big brother.
    Audience: Ages 3-10.
    LCCN 2001130910
    ISBN 0-9666199-2-7

    1. Sibling rivalry–Juvenile fiction. 2. Brothers and sisters–Juvenile fiction. 3. Infants–Juvenile fiction. [1. Sibling rivalry–Fiction. 2. Brothers and sisters--Fiction. 3. Babies–Fiction.] I. Title.

PZ8.3.R1446Jer 2002        [E]
                    QB101-701032
Printed in China

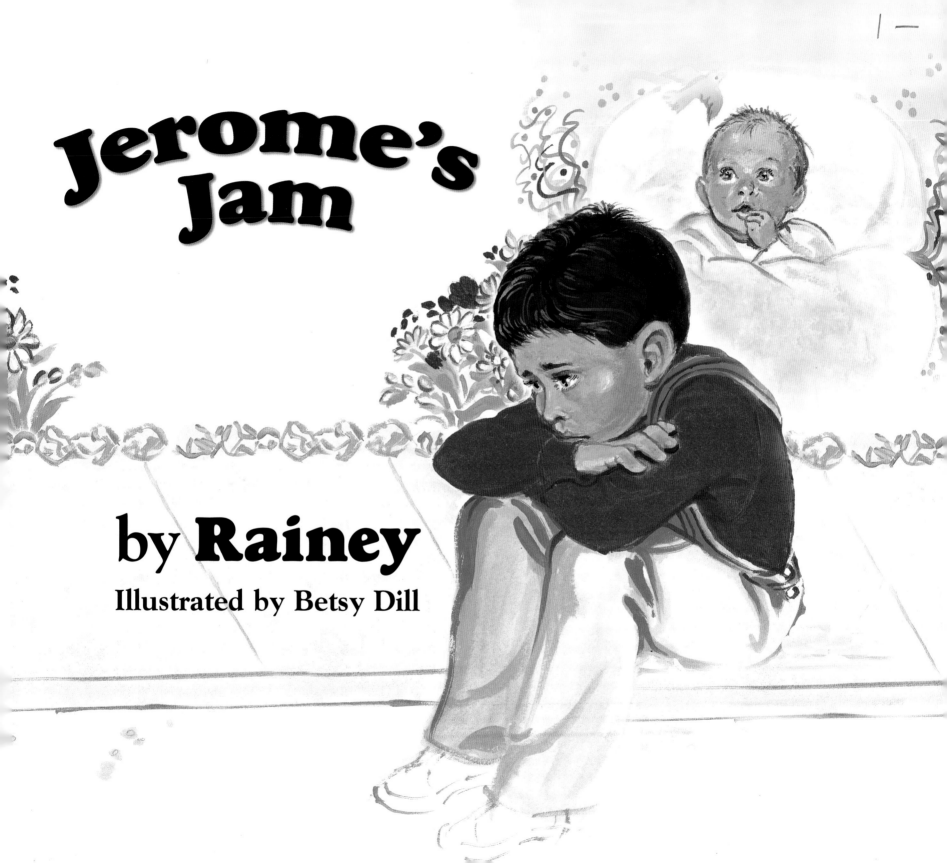

# Jerome's Jam

## by Rainey

Illustrated by Betsy Dill

Every day Jerome would watch her tummy grow.
"Why are you getting so big, Mommy?" he wanted to know.
"I'm having another baby, I hope just like you.
When it comes to children, I've always wanted two."

"But," Jerome asked, "why do we need another?
I don't want a little sister or a brother.
I like having you and Daddy all to myself."
He pouted and leaned on the kitchen shelf.

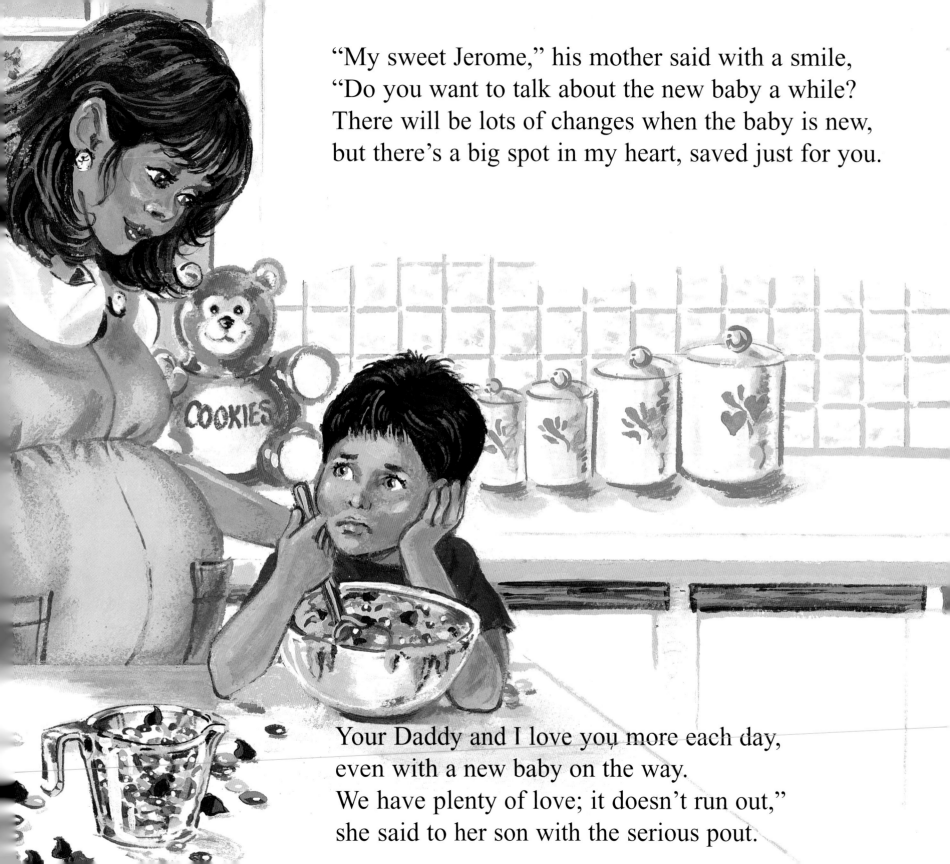

"My sweet Jerome," his mother said with a smile,
"Do you want to talk about the new baby a while?
There will be lots of changes when the baby is new,
but there's a big spot in my heart, saved just for you.

Your Daddy and I love you more each day,
even with a new baby on the way.
We have plenty of love; it doesn't run out,"
she said to her son with the serious pout.

So, off to his room he went with a frown.
It seemed his whole world had turned upside down.

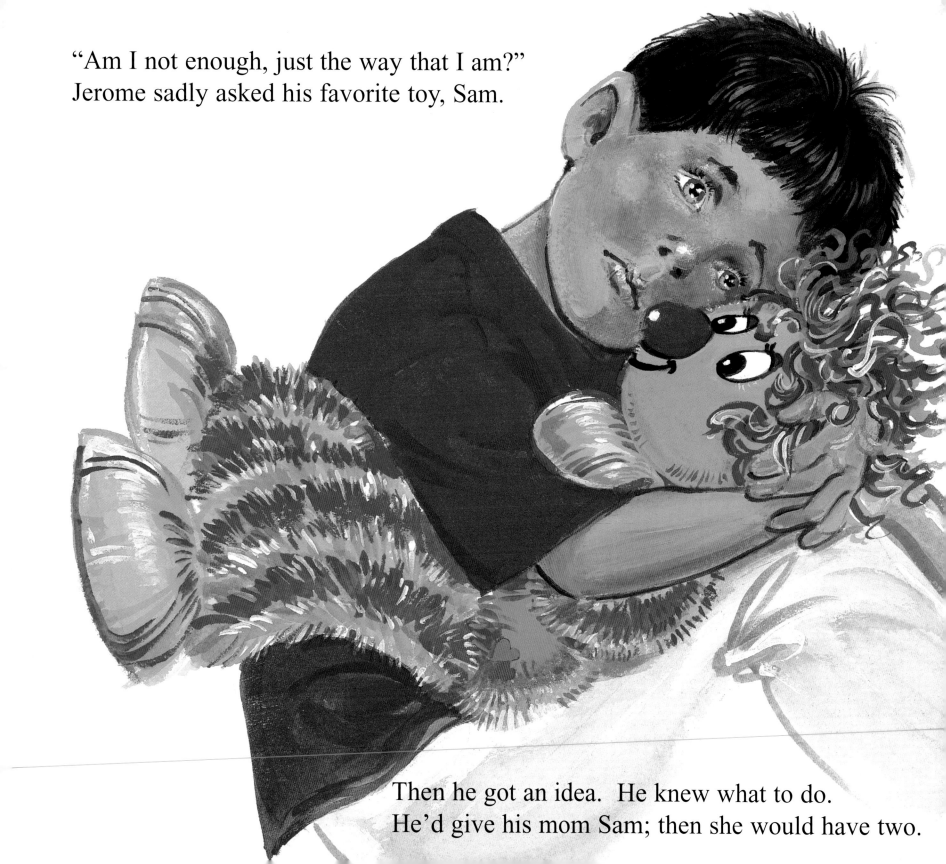

"Am I not enough, just the way that I am?"
Jerome sadly asked his favorite toy, Sam.

Then he got an idea.  He knew what to do.
He'd give his mom Sam; then she would have two.

With Sam behind his back, he walked down the hall.
And when his mother saw him, he looked oh-so-small.

"I liked it before, just you, Daddy and me.
That's the perfect number"— he held up a three.

"Don't worry, my little one, I'll love you even more
when our family reaches the number four."

"If it's four that you want, then you can have Sam,"
and he held out his buddy to get out of this jam.
His mommy reached out and hugged him so tight.
Jerome hugged her back with all of his might.

"Nobody on earth could ever take your place,"
she cooed, wiping tears from Jerome's little face.

"It's okay you're concerned, but I promise you this:
You're my favorite 'Little Man,'" she said with a kiss.
"This baby will love you like Daddy and me.
It'll be all right, just you wait and see."

Time kept on passing; you can't slow it down.
Then his grandma came in from out of town.
His parents kissed him good-bye then they all hugged each other.
"Jerome," they said together, "you'll be the best big brother."

Their car drove off; he watched it go.
He waved and smiled, just for show.

Jerome was really angry and scuffing his feet
when he saw Jazz the DreamDog coming down the street.
She was the magic doggie in the neighborhood
who always appeared when things weren't so good.

He called Jazz over and told her his fear
as down his cheek rolled one big tear.
"My Mommy's having a baby later today.
I get to go to the hospital to meet her and play.

But, I don't want this baby; I've told her before,
and I said it again as she went out the door.
That's when she said she loved me and not to worry.
She had to leave fast 'cause they were in a hurry."

He explained his worries and Jazz listened well,
every once in a while, wagging her tail.
"That new baby will be perfect and tiny and sweet.
They'll think she's so special from her head to her feet.

If it's a baby they want, I'll crawl and talk 'baby talk,'"
he said drawing faces with frowns with his chalk.
Jazz noticed Jerome was starting to mumble.
He was still fussing and starting to grumble.

Just then, Jerome's grandmother called, "Time for a nap."
Jazz followed him inside and climbed into his lap.
Jazz thought to herself, "We only have a few hours.
Time for me to use my magic DreamDog powers!"

When Jerome hugged Jazz, it calmed him down,
changing to a smile what had once been a frown.
He cuddled up to Jazz and took a nap too;
it seemed like the very best thing to do.

And, of course, Jerome had a special dream.
It was all part of the DreamDog scheme.
In his dream, Jerome saw his baby sister.
He touched her tiny head, then bent down and kissed her.

"Because she's so small, she'll need her big brother.
You could help out your dad and your mother."
Jerome realized, by the time the dream was done,
that being the "Big Brother" would be lots of fun.

"She'll think you can do everything and that you're a star.
You can paint, run, count numbers or honk-honk like a car!
She'll look up to you right from the start.
Big brothers are loved deep in the heart.

At first she may cry a lot and be kinda scared.
But remember, that God decided that you should be paired.
She is the one who was picked just for you,
so be sweet to your little sister, whatever you do."

And when Jerome awoke, it was with a smile.
He had been asleep for quite a while.

Jazz said, "Jerome, everything will be all right."
"I know that now," he answered and hugged her tight.

The next day when Jerome got home from school,
he saw the car was back and said, "Oh cool!"
Into his home, he marched with a stride
hoping to find his mother inside.

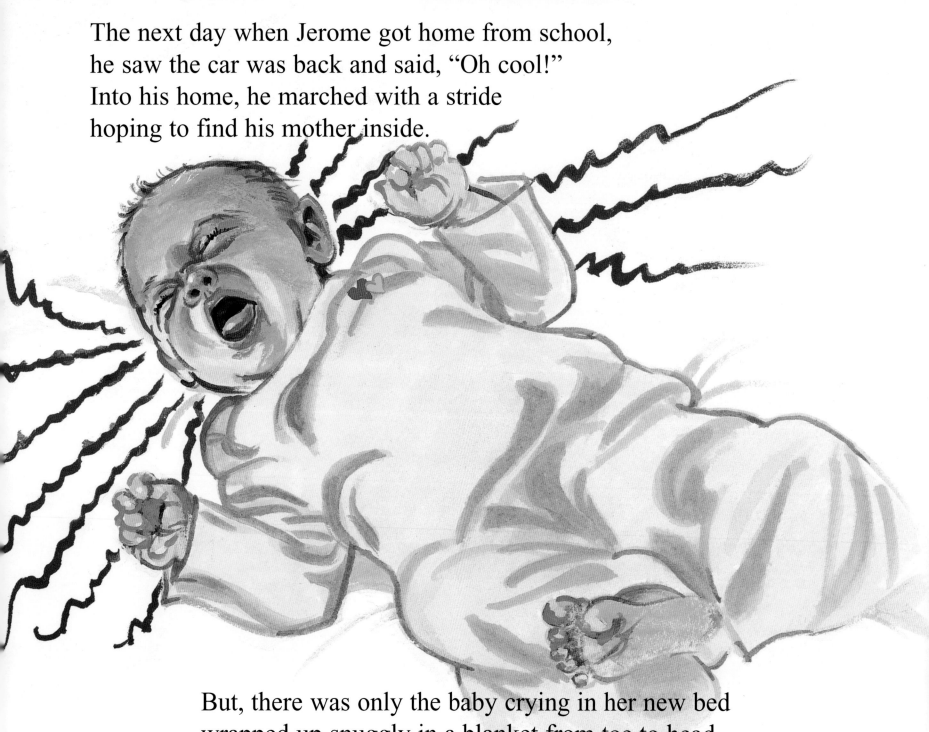

But, there was only the baby crying in her new bed
wrapped up snuggly in a blanket from toe to head.
He remembered his dream and held her tiny hand;
"There's got to be a way to make her understand."

"Don't cry baby sister; don't be sad.
I promise you living here won't be so bad.
I like to play and run and sing;
I can do most anything.

So you've got a playmate when you get big."
And to stop her from crying, he oinked like a pig.

Pretending to be a dog, he growled and said, "Ruff!"

Then acted like a kitten with all of its fluff.

He neighed like a horsie and chirped like a bird.
And from way in the kitchen, his mother heard.

But the baby just kept crying and boo-hoo-hooing no matter what her big brother was doing.

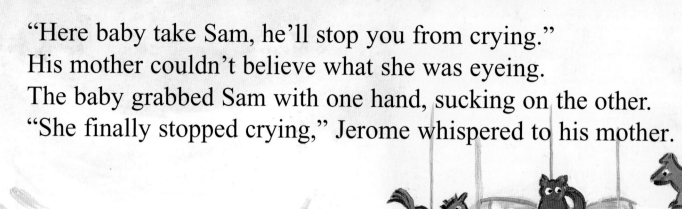

"Here baby take Sam, he'll stop you from crying."
His mother couldn't believe what she was eyeing.
The baby grabbed Sam with one hand, sucking on the other.
"She finally stopped crying," Jerome whispered to his mother.

Now it was Mommy who had tears in her eyes,
but it was just one of her "happy cries."

Later that night when Daddy came home,
he said he was proud of his little Jerome.

Giving his sister his favorite toy
made him quite a special boy.

"It was nice of you to share, but it's only to borrow.
We'll get baby her own 'Sam' tomorrow."

"But you see," Jerome said, "I got something too –
a new baby sister from Mommy and you.
Jazz was right; she already loves me and knows who I am.
I'm her Big Brother who gave her my Sam."

Then they all went in to tell baby goodnight,
and in her little hand, she held Sam so tight.

Now it was time for Jerome to go to bed;
first his bath, then favorite books to be read.
But the best part was being tucked in with kisses
from Mommy and Daddy and hearing their wishes.

"May your dreams always be as sweet as you are,
our sharing, caring Big Brother Superstar."
Jerome felt so loved that his face seemed to beam,
and he cuddled up to Jazz for a special good night dream.

# Note to Parents

**Congratulations on the arrival of your new baby!** What an exciting time this is for you and your entire family, and what a major time for transition and change. Your family dynamic has and will continue to change to include your new member, and roles that previously existed will naturally shift. As with any major transitions in their lives, our children will need our help adapting and adjusting to their new sibling. This story is intended to help your older children look forward to the newest family member's arrival, understand their exciting new role, and know that your baby means more love for the entire family, not less. There are many things we can do to ease this transition, such as:

**Prepare your child for his/her new baby.** Explain in realistic terms what changes will occur when the baby arrives. Tell your child that new babies cry a lot – when they are tired, hungry, hot or cold, have a wet diaper, need to be cuddled, or sometimes just because they are babies. Setting up realistic expectations will help them through this challenging, exhilarating time. And, always refer to the baby as "ours" to let your older child have ownership in the arrival of your new family member.

**Reassure them of your love.** In the story, Jerome's mother says: "There will be lots of changes when the baby is new, but there's a big spot in my heart saved just for you." It is so important to keep reminding your older children how special they are to you, how much you love them, and how there is no one that could ever take their place in your heart and in your life. Say "I understand" when they complain about so much attention going to the baby. Lots of extra hugs and cuddles are a definite must!

**Create a loving environment where your child can discuss concerns.** Being heard is probably the most crucial thing you can do to help your child with the transition. And, understand that jealousy is universal. All children experience it in some manner. It is not a predictor of how well your children will relate to each other in later years. But, we do know that if children are not allowed, and even encouraged, to express negative feelings, these feelings will come out in non-productive ways. Help your child talk through any negative feelings about the baby. This may be difficult for you to hear, but it is much better than the alternative. Anger, jealousy and confusion when kept inside can turn into violence. Children will find a way to express these feelings, through either physical or emotional outlets, if safe spaces for communicating these ideas are not created.

**Avoid comparisons.** We want to allow our children to be and become their own special selves. Highlight your children's unique gifts and mirror those back to them so they can see and be proud of their own talents and qualities. Comparisons are just one of the ways we can cause jealousy and anger. Be aware of your actions and words; children are very sensitive during times of change.

**Tell your older children how much you will need their help.** Explain that babies need lots of extra attention because they can't do anything for themselves. They need help eating, getting dressed, bathing – and with all of these activities the big brother/sister can help. Giving them responsibility with the new baby makes them feel special and a part of the new energy around the baby. Don't make the mistake of building an artificial wall between the baby and the older sibling in an effort to protect the new baby. Instead, broaden your already existing family circle to allow for your new member. Don't shut out the older siblings, but allow them to nurture, cuddle, rock, feed and even help with changing diapers for the baby.

**Set aside special "alone time" for you and your older child without the baby.** Have your husband, a friend, or a sitter watch the baby and take your older child out for special times (to the park, to get ice cream or for a walk — just the two of you). Also, use the baby's naptime to read, sing, dance, play, and talk to your older child. Time alone will be crucial to your child's self-esteem. Create time alone with each of your children to let them know how important they are to you.

**Allow your older child to keep special toys and clothes.** Seeing all your toys disappear into the baby's room can cause anger and jealousy. Know that your older child may have outgrown certain toys but still be very attached to others (stuffed animals in particular). In the story, Jerome gives the baby his favorite stuffed toy. His father is quick to tell him how proud he is of his sharing "but it's only to borrow…we'll get baby her own Sam tomorrow."

**Reinforce the special things about being older.** In the story, Jazz lists activities that Jerome can do. Try to point out your children's accomplishments and lavish praise on them. Reinforcing all the good things they do is extremely important at a time that will be full of "don'ts." It is only natural that there will be many negative rules that will be established (Don't scream around the baby, Don't pull the baby's arms, etc.), but remember to focus on the positives.

**Be careful when assigning new roles.** Overnight, your child's role has changed in the family. Don't expect him to grow up overnight just because he is the big brother. Many children revert to younger behaviors when the baby arrives and want you to call them baby, too. Knowing that this is perfectly normal (and only temporary) will help you deal with their changes.

**Try not to fuss over the baby in front of your other child.** There will be enough relatives lavishing attention on the baby and plenty of time for that when your older child is not present. You should talk to your child about all the attention that the baby will get. Let your older child know that you understand how he feels with all the attention going to someone else.

**And, be prepared for your heart to burst with more love than you could ever imagine.** When my son walked around the maternity ward telling everyone: "I'm a Big Brother," or the first time he told the new baby "I love you," or the first time he sang him to sleep — you could never imagine that you could feel so much love. This is where the book helps teach our children how to "Find the Heart." As in Jazz the DreamDog's first adventure, there is a hidden heart on each page, but this time they represent the interlocking hearts of your children. Good luck, get some sleep, share your joy, and help your children discover the magic within themselves!